The Gecko

Nigel Clayton

The Gecko
Nigel Clayton

Published in Australia by Zuytdorp Press, 2026

The Gecko
ISBN 978-0-6456465-7-3

BISAC
JUV002000   JUVENILE FICTION / Animals / General
JUV008050   JUVENILE FICTION / Comics & Graphic Novels / Animals
JUV070000   JUVENILE FICTION / Poetry (see also Stories in Verse)

Other Titles by this Author
- specifically for kids -

The Wizard of Oz in Verse
The Itsy-Bitsy [available in hardcover and paperback]
A Turtle Named Myrtle
A Pygmy Possum Named Henry
The Legend of Waterfall Creek
The Last Bunyip
The Kookaburra

Available from most online book stores
- or -
www.zuytdorpbooks.com [if still active]

The Gecko

Oh, the back garden, so quiet and peaceful,
No dangers seen, nothing about too harmful,
With a weeping willow growing so very tall,
With shrubs all about, some large, some small.

The Gecko

The Gecko

A crow was then quite suddenly seen,

Flying aloft the garden, for a meal, very keen,

He was clearly hunting, on the search for food,

For something nourishing, he was in the mood.

The Gecko

The Gecko

There it was, the crow saw it, plain as day,

Saw movement down below, not so far away,

Just a quick flap of the wings, that was all,

And the crow did caw, made his call.

The Gecko

The Gecko

Down he came, swooping so very fast,

To take of a meal which would not last,

It was but a small snack and nothing more,

But food was food, too good to ignore.

The Gecko

It was a worm, a worm for the taking,

The crow grabbed at it, his head shaking,

He lifted his head up, pulled the worm in,

And swallowed it whole, with an inward grin.

The Gecko

In that same garden was a small gecko,

His way around this garden, he did know,

He knew all the hiding spots, good and bad,

And knew where the best insects were to be had.

The Gecko

The Gecko

The gecko snatched onto a flying insect,

He did so quickly, and with great effect,

He too was quick to draw his food in,

He too was satisfied and gave an inward grin.

The Gecko

Suddenly the gecko saw the crow standing there,
In the middle of the garden, eating his fare,
And the crow looked up, seeing the gecko as well,
Yet the gecko was too far away to comfortably smell.

The Gecko

The crow stood there for a moment, to be sure,
Realising quickly, that for his hunger, it was a cure,
A big fat gecko, ready to be eaten, every bit,
And so to the security of this meal, the crow did commit.

The Gecko

The Gecko

The gecko saw the crow looking, staring hard,

Right there in the garden, that lovely backyard,

For a moment it seemed that everything did pause,

And both the crow and the gecko, knew the cause.

The Gecko

The Gecko

They had attracted each others attention,
The gecko deciding to run, there no other option,
Run or be eaten, that was the choice, no more,
Yet the gecko knew not, what was in store.

The Gecko

The Gecko

The gecko turned then, jumped from the bush,

Ran as fast as he could, as the wind about did whoosh,

He ran as though there was no tomorrow,

And upon his great speed, he did have to borrow.

The Gecko

Run, run run, don't look back,

Stop now and you become a crow's snack,

Whatever you do, do not stop running,

Keep those legs pumping, keep them moving.

The Gecko

The crow saw the gecko move and then leapt,

He jumped into the air, in this, his attempt,

A great effort to try and secure that meal,

From the gecko, his very life, to crush, to steal.

The Gecko

The Gecko

Yet the gecko managed to get away,

To safety he did manage, and without delay,

To a rock formation that he knew well,

Yet the crow was still coming, this he could tell.

The Gecko

He could hear the crow move through the air,

The gecko's hearing being rather acute, as was fair,

And there the gecko did stay, beneath the rock,

And he laughed to himself, the crow to mock.

The Gecko

The crow landed near, seeing the gecko's head,

The situation with the rock formation easily read,

There was no way he would get his meal now,

Hence the gecko's victory, he did allow.

The Gecko

The Gecko

But wait, the gecko could quite easily be smelt,

And in the crow's mouth he would simply melt,

The gecko's eyes could be seen clear enough,

So the crow decided, to then and there, be rough.

The Gecko

The Gecko

The crow tried to peck at the gecko so hidden,

But he was out of reach, as though forbidden,

There was no way the gecko would budge,

Of character the crow was a good judge.

The Gecko

The Gecko

The crow decided to fly up and away,
He could not truly afford to linger, to stay,
There was other food to be had, to be sure,
But he would watch the gecko, it later to lure.

The Gecko

The Gecko

But the crow would not receive any immediate chance,
And the gecko looked about, here and there he did glance,
Yes, making sure the coast was clear, before he did run,
To further safety and home, away from the midday sun.

The Gecko

Yes, yes, it was clear now, run, run very fast,

And at his great speed, all would be aghast,

He ran across an open area, to get to the other side,

And once there he would have somewhere to hide.

The Gecko

The gecko ran across some hot, flat stone,
All by himself, undoubtedly all alone,
And then he felt a vibration, from upon the ground,
On turning his head, the source was found.

The Gecko

The Gecko

It was a human boy, with a jar in his hand,
He was running along, that flat piece of land,
The boy was out to catch the gecko, to imprison him,
And rather suddenly, the gecko did become grim.

The Gecko

The Gecko

The boy did not stop, and chased that gecko fast,
That huge, monstrous boy, with stamina to last,
That beastly boy with long arms, with fingers and thumbs,
His heart beating fast, as fast as a dozen drums.

The Gecko

The gecko hid quickly, but not in a good spot,
And the boy grabbed hold of him: "Ah, ha; jackpot."
The gecko was thrust into the jar, it cealed with a lid,
And escape he could not, no matter what he did.

The Gecko

The boy carried the gecko in the jar, to a table,

And wherever the gecko looked, all was visible,

For the jar was made of glass, which he knew little about,

It was an invisible shield, and all he wanted was to get out.

The Gecko

The Gecko

So there he waited, the heat of the sun beating down,
The situation made him sad, and hence he did frown,
Moisture was growing within the glass cage,
And he was filled with a great grief, and much rage.

The Gecko

The Gecko

How much longer could he last, this he thought,

Before release from the heat, could be sought,

The heat growing worse and worse, it growing hotter,

That kid had placed him there, that ginormous monster.

The Gecko

Beads of water were running down the glass,

He smelt a food stuff, on which he wished to pass,

For the smell was awful, not good at all,

And when he tried to climb, he did quickly fall.

The Gecko

Meanwhile the crow was flying up high,

He looked about whilst flying, and gave a sigh,

He wished to have something more, something good,

And he knew that if he searched, he surely would.

The Gecko

The Gecko

And there is was, on the table, in the garden,

The gecko was in a jar: ah, an opportunity most golden,

The crow quickly flew down and landed next to the jar,

That gecko couldn't run now, could not run far.

The Gecko

The Gecko

The crow looked and tried to peck the gecko,
Of glass jars, even he, had no experience, he did not know,
He knew not how to get inside such thing as this… cage,
This jar upon table, upon this wooden, open stage.

The Gecko

The Gecko

Try and try he did to peck through the glass,

But he could not get through, the gecko to harass,

And the lid, a solid object, covering the jar's top,

Even that put his efforts to a complete stop.

The Gecko

And then the jar moved, it toppled slightly,

And the crow pecked harder still, rather smartly,

The jar wobbled and wobbled, and then fell over,

Falling down upon the ground, upon grass and clover.

The Gecko

The gecko was free, now was his chance,
He didn't even make opportunity for a backwards glance,
He just ran and ran, refusing to look, refusing to stop,
Of his energy within, he would not spare a single drop.

The Gecko

The Gecko

Into a bush he disappeared, before the crow saw,
The crow knew not where he went, and he did caw,
He was so unhappy, the gecko had gotten away,
What could the crow do now, what could he possibly say?

The Gecko

The Gecko

The gecko waited a little while before then testing the air,
All appeared clear, but he was still filled with despair,
He flicked out his tongue, several more times to be sure,
He was no longer in a situation, one so grave and poor.

The Gecko

The Gecko

He gecko ran off again, to the next hiding spot he knew,
Back to where the crow had annoyed him, as they do,
He hid there for a short period and tasted the air again,
Before running off one more time, his excitement to contain.

The Gecko

The Gecko

He ran and ran the long distance to his home's entrance,
And stopped momentarily before he did, further advance,
For he didn't wish, a certain gecko, to know of his ordeal,
His dreadful day he wished to hide, of it, wished to conceal.

The Gecko

The Gecko

The gecko stepped off, one final time, or so he did hope,
Walking slowly and with purpose, down the slight slope,
Right into the openness, there beneath the ground,
That place where life was lived, where joy could be found.

The Gecko

The Gecko

Coming to view was the one he loved most of all,
And greeting her he could not, for a moment, stall,
He pulled up in front of her and they said their hello,
Right there in the open, beneath the ground, far below.

The Gecko

The Gecko

The gecko and his wife, the wife and her eggs seven,
Loved conquered all, and that was here proven,
For the gecko felt no more fear, felt pure joy instead,
And the horrors of his day, would forever go unread.

The Gecko

The Gecko

The gecko would never tell the wife of his dreadful day,
Besides, what exactly was it that he could possibly say,
That a boy was being mean, placed him in a burning cage,
No, no; he was happy now, and no longer filled with rage.

The Gecko

THE END

* 9 7 8 0 6 4 5 6 4 6 5 7 3 *